Charlie the Bat
Saves Halloween

ISBN 978-1-63814-454-0 (Paperback)
ISBN 978-1-63814-455-7 (Hardcover)
ISBN 978-1-63814-456-4 (Digital)

Covenant Books, Inc.
11661 Hwy 707
Murrells Inlet, SC 29576
www.covenantbooks.com

Charlie the Bat Saves Halloween

Timothy Babcock

In the state of Massachusetts, there was a forming community of Europeans who had settled in a small place named Salem. Old Salem was becoming a quaint little community, and it rested in the banks near the harbor.

The month is October, and the days were chilly and much chillier at night. The trees were almost bare, and the ground was scattered with leaves of yellows, reds, and oranges. In the small village of Salem, the people were preparing for the coming winter months.

The small community was also preparing for the yearly October holiday, Halloween. They were setting out carved pumpkins on their porches and hanging scary ghosts.

Far off in the countryside of Old Salem, there was a decrepit old house up on a hill. There was a long gravel road that led up to the house. The house was old, unpainted, and broken. Shingles were missing on the roof, and the window shutters were hanging this way and that way.

Oh, what a sight it was. It was such a sight that the hairs on the back of your neck would scream out of fear. Anyone who dared gander at the house for more than a minute was considered the bravest of souls.

Inside the house, there lived a witch. Kathy Cackle, many called her, because, most nights after the big yellow moon rose into the sky, you could hear her dry and rough cackle from miles around. Kathy the witch was short and round. She wore a black cloak that dragged all over the ground.

Under her cloak, she wore a tattered and ripped old brown dress, with patches here and patches there. Her shoes were worn old leather, and her socks were bright orange with purple stripes. The witch's hat was large and black, with a rim that was big enough to set a magic candle on. Her hat tapered off to a point at the very tip.

Kathy Cackle did not live alone in the house. Kathy had a cat named Stinker and two bats, one named Charlie and the other named Tina. A broom, the witch called Mr. Bristles. And a mouse, he had the most peculiar name of all. His name was Cheese. They made up the finest of scary crew for a witch in her house.

Stinker, the cat, was mostly black, but he had white paws and a white tip at the end of his tail. Stinker had big bright-green eyes and an old shoelace for a necklace. On the necklace, he had himself a little name tag made from worn old copper.

Tina the bat was well-kept. She was small enough to hide in a shoe. Tina had on a little red cape, and she was immensely proud of her little red cape. Charlie the bat was a tad bit bigger than Tina but not by a lot.

Charlie had on his head a few hairs that went in different directions. On one of his wild hairs, the witch had tied a bell. The bell would help the crew keep track of Charlie whenever he got lost in the house.

Mr. Bristles, the broom, looked like most brooms. His handle was long and brown. His bristles were held tight to his handle with tight wrapped wire, and his bristles were all curved in one direction near the bottom. Cheese, the mouse, was tiny and gray. He had on a small pair of brown booties and a bib made from an old shirt wrapped around his little neck.

The people, or their children, rarely ventured up the old road to the house. The witch's house could be seen from the town, way off in the distance. The townsfolk would stop occasionally and look up at the hill and the house. But that was all most people ever did.

As night would fall on Salem, the people would gather up their children and run into their houses and lock their doors. The sky would get dark, and the moon would rise.

The owls would hoot here and hoot over there. The dead fall leaves would blow this way and that way. It began to get chilly at night, and fires were burning in the fireplaces. Scarecrows adorned the dried-up cornfields, and ghosts and jack-o'-lanterns stood watch on people's porches.

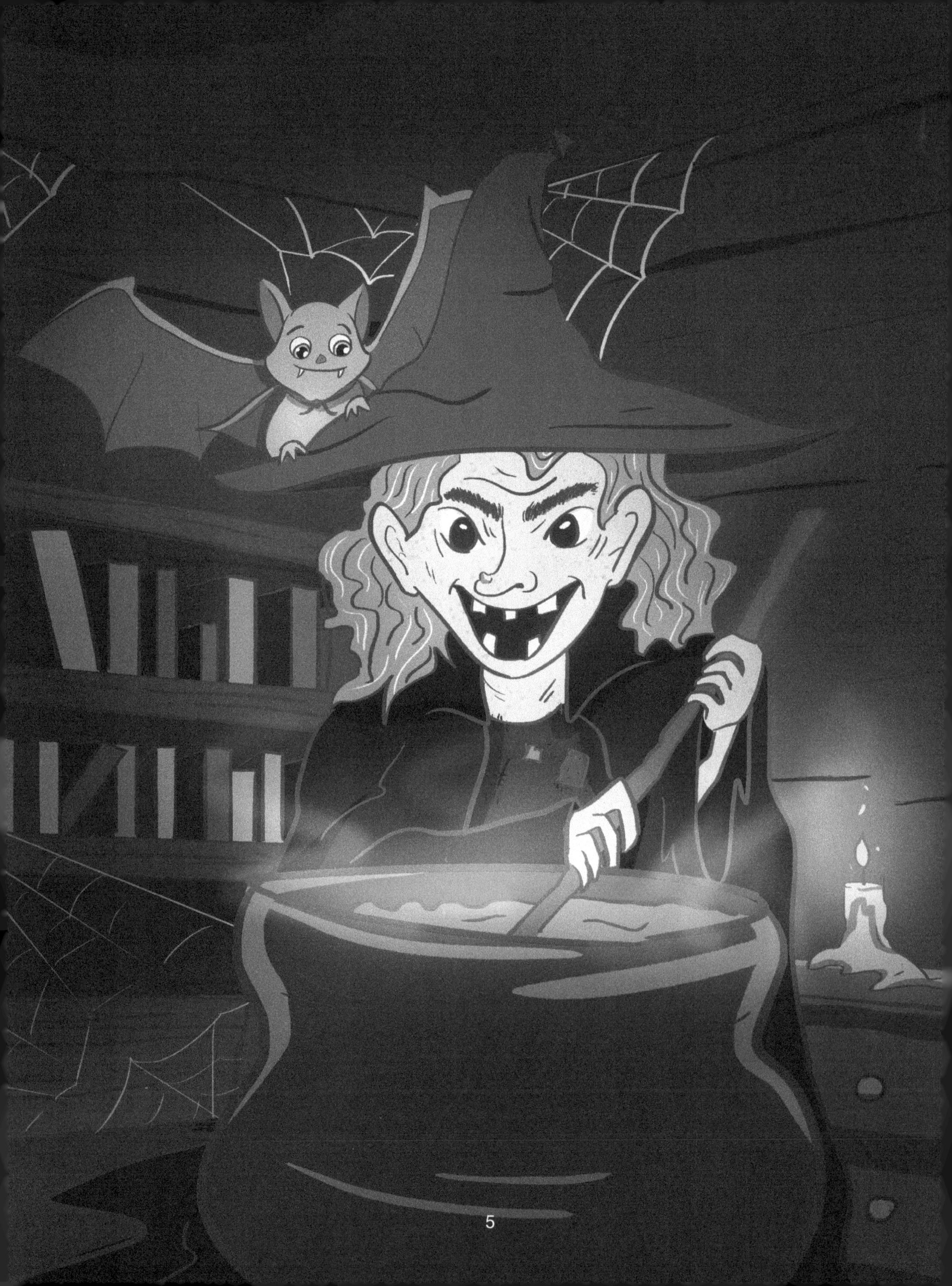

Up on the old hill, in the terrible house, there was much activity. Kathy was busy mixing her brews and casting her spells. From down in the village, people could see smoke coming from the chimney of the house.

Sometimes the smoke was blue; other times, it was orange. Sometimes on special nights, the smoke was pitch-black, and when it rose out of the old chimney, it would scream with such a fright.

The people in the village would huddle and hold one another tight. In the old house of the witch, Mr. Bristles the broom would move about, sweeping here and then over there. The mouse, whose name was Cheese, would beg and beg for a piece of cheese.

Tina the bat spent most of her time nestled upon the witch's hat. Charlie the bat would hiss and fuss. Charlie would get caught up in the spiderwebs that adorned corners in the house. Other times, Charlie got stuck in the witch's socks that were hanging up to dry.

"Charlie!" the witch would yell. "Why are you in my socks?" the witch would ask. Charlie would wiggle and waggle, and soon he was out of the old witches' socks. Charlie would flutter around upside down and, sometimes, inside down. Mr. Bristles the broom and Tina the bat and Cheese the mouse would laugh and laugh.

Stinker the cat would tip his head and say, "You're a silly bat, Charlie." Kathy the witch was not in the mood for Charlie's accidents.

"I try to be a good bat," Charlie would say.

All that night, the witch kept busy with witch things.

Soon it became daylight, and the people in the village of Salem went out and did all the things that people in a village did. The men went to work, and the wives cleaned and made bread.

The children went off to school to learn about numbers and writing. They learned about the alphabet too. Up on the hill, in the old house, the witch and her friends were sleeping. They had been up the night before, doing things that they ought not.

Charlie the bat, though, was wide-awake. He was ravaging through the old cupboards, searching for crumbs of cookies and rotten old apples. When he found something that suited him, he would sit in the darkest of corners and eat.

Mr. Bristles the broom would awaken every so often when he heard Charlie rustling around. "Why don't you sleep like the rest of us?" Mr. Bristles asked. Charlie would stop eating long enough to give the broom the sourest of sourest looks.

Tina the bat lay on the witch's hat sound asleep. Kathy the witch was sleeping too. Kathy snored, and every time she snored, her shoes would untie themselves and then tie themselves back up again. Stinker the cat was sound asleep too, dreaming of things only a cat would dream about.

Cheese the mouse was sleeping in his little mouse house. He was dreaming of the biggest pieces of cheese. As he dreamed about the cheese, his little whiskers would wiggle and wiggle. All was quiet in the old witch's house.

The day was beginning to end, and the people and their children began to end their activities for the day. As the sun went down and the sky grew dark, the people began to retire to their houses. Kathy the witch began to stir, and she stretched her arms and opened her eyes.

A new night of witchery had come. The broom began to yawn and wiggle his bristles. Tina the bat began to wake up, and she stretched her bat wings. Cheese the mouse woke up also and instantly started searching for food to nibble on.

As everyone started moving about in the old house on the hill, they noticed that Charlie the bat was unaccounted for. "Where is Charlie?" Kathy asked. Everyone in the house began to look in the cupboards, under the chairs, and in the corners.

Nowhere could Charlie be found. While everyone was still asleep, Charlie had snuck up the chimney and out onto the house's roof. Charlie wanted to go to the village to see what the people were doing.

Once in the village, Charlie noticed that children were outside, playing. It had not gotten late enough yet for children to be in bed. Halloween was fast approaching, and the children were outside, playing games. They were playing hide-and-seek and scaring one another for fun.

Charlie sat in a tree nearby and watched the children play. Charlie enjoyed this very much. Charlie was not interested in casting spells or working for the witch. The children would take turns hiding behind the trees while the others searched for the ones who were hiding.

Charlie would sit on the branches of the trees and giggle with joy. He wanted to play with the children, too, but he was afraid that he would scare the children away. "I would love to play with the children," Charlie would say.

As the children continued to play, Charlie looked on intently. He was overcome with joy to be able to sit and watch the children play. As the night grew even later, the children began to congregate on their porches.

They would play with the Halloween decorations that hung about the porch. They would also gather around the jack-o'-lanterns and watch the small candles burn inside them.

Meanwhile, up on the old hill in the terrible old house, the witch and the broom and the others continued to look for Charlie. "Where could Charlie be?" they would ask one another. They searched high and low in this corner and that corner. And under the table and behind the shoes, nowhere could he be found.

Back in the village of Salem, the children began to be called inside for the night by their parents. So Charlie gathered himself up and began to prepare to return to the house on the hill. Charlie knew that he might get a scolding once he arrived back home, but he was not worried. He was happy and very satisfied with his night's activities.

Charlie took flight from the tree and flew into the night sky. As he flew, he looked at the clouds and the moon that took refuge behind them. Charlie arrived back at the house and climbed down the chimney.

Charlie emerged from the fireplace a bit dirty and covered in ash. He looked at everyone standing in front of the fireplace and giggled nervously. "Where have you been, little bat?" Kathy the witch asked.

Charlie replied, "I have been in the village, watching the children play." The witch shook her head in disgust. "If you're going to go down to that village, you have to frighten the children!" she said.

Mr. Bristles the broom nodded, in agreement with the witch. The mouse and the cat and Tina the bat laughed at Charlie once more. "You are such a peculiar bat." they said. Charlie looked back at them with sadness on his little face.

"But I love the children. I cannot frighten them," Charlie answered. The witch and her crew went back to doing the things that they were doing, stirring brew in the cauldron and chanting and singing.

The witch stood over the cauldron, dropping in dead flies and spiderwebs. Kathy then ran outside and grabbed a rock. She went back inside and threw it in the cauldron. "A rock will add a special flavor," she said.

Mr. Bristles went close to the cauldron; he grabbed some of his bristles, broke them off, and threw them in. Stinker the cat wanted to add to the brew, too, so he plucked some cat hair from his tail and threw it in the cauldron.

"Ah, the brew is almost ready," Kathy the witch proclaimed. The broom, the mouse, and the others asked the witch what she was going to do with the brew. Kathy the witch turned and looked at her crew. "I am going to make a gift to the people in the village," she replied.

The broom, the cat, and the others jumped for joy. Kathy the witch continued to say, "This gift will make them afraid to come outside." Then Kathy the witch looked at Charlie. "You will never see those terrible children again!" she yelled.

Charlie looked in surprise at the witch.

"Why do you have to be so terrible?" he asked.

Kathy replied with a snarling grin, "A witch is not a witch if she is not terrible."

Charlie the bat looked down to the dirty floor and began to cry. He covered his little face with his bat wings and sobbed and sobbed some more. The brew in the cauldron was simmering, and bubbles would pop. Kathy would take the wooden stick and churn the brew more.

The cat, the mouse, and Tina the bat watched the brew as it bubbled and stewed. Stinker the cat went to lie down under the window. He had decided that it was time to wash up. Cheese the mouse went to his little mouse house and began to nibble on a small piece of leftover cheese.

Mr. Bristles the broom went about doing what a broom should do. He went about sweeping up dust bunnies and dirt from the floor. Meanwhile, Kathy stood watch over the special brew. Sometimes the brew would bubble over the sides of the cauldron. The brew would run down the sides of the cauldron and touch the flames, and the flames would hiss and snap.

Kathy the witch would sit on her stool and watch the brew. Sometimes the brew was green, and sometimes it would turn yellow. The brew was ready now, and the witch began to gather up small jars to put the brew in.

She went about gathering lids for the small jars to. Kathy was planning on delivering the brew herself to the people of the village.

"I will make it look like a peace offering," Kathy said. The witch thought, if she did that, the people would be more likely to accept her gift. Kathy began to pour the brew into the jars one by one until all the jars were full. Then each jar she closed with the lids.

Kathy then grabbed an old wicker basket from her shelves and began to put the jars of the brew into the basket. "This will make a delightful stew for their supper." Kathy giggled. The witch got herself ready for the trip into Salem, and the cat and the bats and the broom and the mouse were going too.

They were all together going to go down the hill into the village. Charlie the bat did not want to go along with them. He was not happy about what he was seeing.

Charlie thought quickly, rubbing his little wings on his head. "I think that the people might now be in their beds," Charlie said. Kathy the witch ran to her windows and gazed down over the hill to the village. From her window, she could see that there was still some light shining through the windows of the cottages.

"The children might be in bed, but the grown-ups are still stirring." Kathy giggled. "We shall leave now," the witch continued. So out the door went the witch and her crew, but Charlie stayed behind. He did not want to be a part of the witch's deeds. As the witch and her crew descended the hill, Charlie watched through the windows of the old house on the hill.

Pretty soon, the witch and her crew arrived in the village. They went to the first cottage they found and went up to the door. Kathy raised her wrinkled old hand and began to knock on the door. A young woman opened the door and began to scream with fright.

"Please go away from here," the young woman pleaded. And with that, the door slammed shut. So the witch left and made her way through the dried-up leaves and on down the path to the next cottage. Once at the cottage, Kathy began to knock on the door.

A young man answered the door and stood with a stare like no other on his face. "What do you want, old witch?" he asked.

Kathy thought for a moment before answering. "I have come with a surprise," Kathy said. She reached into her basket and pulled out a jar of brew and raised it to the man. "I have made you a fine stew," Kathy added.

The young man looked at the jar of brew and shook his hand in gesture at it. "I really don't want anything from you," the man said.

Kathy held the jar and moved it higher, saying, "Ah, but this stew is delicious."

The man looked at the jar and then looked at the witch. Kathy continued, "It will warm your innards" The man refused the stew and sent the old witch on her way into the darkness.

From there, the witch and her crew were turned away from every door until all the cottages had been tried. Kathy the witch and her mysterious crew returned to the house on the hill. The wicked plot had expired with no success. Charlie the bat was pleased about the foiled plot. He did not want harm to come to the village folks or their children.

By now it was extremely late into the night, so the witch paced back and forth across her dirty wooden floors. The broom stood in the corner, and the cat lay under the window. Cheese the mouse went scurrying around, looking for food, and Tina the bat sat on the witch's hat. Charlie the bat hung upside down from a rafter with happiness in his heart.

Soon morning came, and the witch and her crew retired to sleep. Once again down in the village, the sun began to rise over the horizon. The men went on their ways to work while the wives cleaned and made house. The children got dressed for school and gathered outside together.

It became another fine day for the families in the village of Salem. Meanwhile, up on the hill in the old house, all was quiet. Everyone inside the house was sleeping. Charlie the bat was asleep too. He looked forward to sneaking out of the house to go and see the children.

In the village, the day was nice with warmth from the sun. It was a particularly warm day, so the women were hanging clothes outside to dry. The women also began to prepare gifts and treats as Halloween was in a few more days. After a while, the children had been let out of school for the day and began to return to their homes.

Throughout the village, you could hear the laughter and chatter of the children as they gathered in front of their homes. The women greeted them with hugs and apples.

The men soon started to go to the village from the places of work. And the village folks gathered in fun and festivities. Wonderful smells came from the village sometimes, and there were smells of fresh baked pies and fresh baked breads.

The smell of smoke rose from the chimneys of the cottages, and somehow, it was warming to the heart. The day carried on with conversations of activities, and plans were made. The children had changed into their play clothes and had gathered outside for games.

The women had begun to take clothes off the clotheslines, and some of the men relaxed on porches with smoke pipes in their mouths. Life was the best it could be in the village. All the children in the village of Salem grew more excited as Halloween rapidly approached.

Up on the hill in the tethered old house, it remained quiet for a time. There was not much stirring in the house other than soft sounds of dreams being dreamed. Cheese the mouse woke up and began to scurry around for tidbits of scattered crumbs on the floor.

Mr. Bristles the broom would move ever so slightly as he slept, brushing his withered bristles against the wood of the floor. Tina the bat became a bit restless in her sleep and turned a bit to get more comfortable. Stinker the cat was snoring away, dreaming of things only a cat would dream about.

Kathy the witch was sound asleep; nobody knew what a witch dreamed about, but every so often, she would stir slightly and let out soft but fiendish cackles. Charlie the bat had found his place for sleep in an old tin cup. He was all curled up in the bottom of the cup ever so cozily.

The entire house remained still because there was more mischief and devising to be had once night had come. The day moved along, and the sun began to lower over the hills of Salem.

As the sun went down, the shadows of the bare trees in the village stretched their arms across the land. As the shadows of the trees reached across the land, they seemed to grab at this thing and that thing. It was a mystifying sight to see. The air grew chilly, and the leaves began to blow this way and that way over the land.

Soon the sun had gone out of sight, and the sky began to turn dark blue. The first of the stars began to appear in the sky as though they were heralding in a new night of mystery. The women and their men had gone inside their cottages, and the women began to prepare supper to eat. The children stayed outside and played with one another.

As the sun retired out of sight, the moon began to rise to take its place in the night sky. The moon was big and yellow, and it was full as it showed itself above the trees. It seemed to smile as its light showed down upon the village of Salem.

Sometimes the children still outside would stop and listen to the wind. The wind blew through the bare branches of the trees, and it seemed to be talking and howling in the strangest of ways.

The children would run and scream in delight, and they would take turns hiding behind this tree or that tree while the rest went in search to find them. Through the lit windows of the cottages, you could see the women moving about.

They were busy setting tables and placing dishes of food. The men of the house could be seen sitting at the tables, moving their hands about in conversations.

Now the women had begun to call their children inside as it was beginning to be quite late for them to be outside. The children had now gone inside, and they began to eat supper along with their families.

There was laughter and conversations about the day's activities. The smells of baked bread and meat dishes filled the air, and the sounds of food being served up and dishes clattering once again filled the hearts of the people with joy.

Back up on the old hill, the witch and her crew of friends began to move about as the night had come again with its mysteries and magical dabbling. The cat and the bats and the mouse gathered close to the witch as she began to think about a new plan for the village people.

Kathy the witch would pace over by the window and think, and then she would pace some more. She would wring her hands together and scratch her head. "There must be something awful I can do to the people down there in that village," she wondered.

Mr. Bristles the broom moved over close to the cauldron and investigated it. "What will we do with this brew?" he asked the witch.

Kathy the witch looked at the brew and then looked at Mr. Bristles. "We surely cannot eat the brew," she said.

Kathy explained that they could not eat the brew because it was made to make people afraid. So with that, the witch and her crew had made the decision to throw the brew away.

So as Kathy the witch continued to devise a new plan, the bats and the cat and the broom and the mouse went about their own activities. Suddenly the silence was broken as the witch lifted her hand in the air and finger pointed up.

"Aha!" the witch yelled. "I know what I'll do." The bats and the cat and the mouse and the broom stopped what they were doing and stared at the witch.

Kathy had decided that she would make all the village people sad, especially the children, by taking away their Halloween festivals. Her plan was to go down into the village once everyone was asleep. Kathy the witch sneered and laughed as she grinned at each one of her friends in the old house.

Kathy the witch looked at each of her friends, saying, "If you each will help me, this can be a great success."

Charlie the bat put his little wings over his mouth in utter surprise. Then Charlie looked at the witch with anger on his face. "I will not help you to be so cruel!" he declared. "Why can't you be a good and kind witch?"

Kathy the witch looked at Charlie with a puzzled look on her face. "Did you ever hear of a good witch?" Charlie looked down to the floor and shook his head. Kathy the witch started planning more about what she would do to ruin Halloween for the villagers. She gave each of her friends an assignment to complete when they went down into the village.

Mr. Bristles was assigned the job of taking all the candy apples, and Stinker the cat was given the job of tearing up all the Halloween decorations that hung on porches. Cheese the mouse was asked to chew up all the jack-o'-lanterns. Tina the bat was given a special job. It was up to her to sit and stand guard while the others ruined Halloween.

Kathy the witch would help where help was needed, of course. She would eat the candy apples and run through the yards with the ghosts that hung on the porch. She would also help Cheese the mouse by stepping on and squishing any carved pumpkins that Cheese did not chew up.

So it was prepared; the awful plot was due to be carried out on Halloween night. Now that everything had been planned, the witch and her crew decided to take the rest of this night for relaxation. Kathy sat down in her chair and began to read her spell-casting books. The others, except for Charlie, lounged around the old house here and there.

Charlie the bat had to do something to stop the witch's plans. He did not want to see the village people sad. He did not want to see the children cry. Charlie had to do something, but what? Charlie went to a dark part of the house, out of sight, away from the others, to think.

The rest of the night carried on, and eventually, the first signs of morning came. The dark-blue night sky began to show lighter blues, and the horizon became a soft light yellow. The birds started to chirp and sing as the sun began to show itself.

As the sun got higher in the sky, it began to cast light on the land, and the glistening blades of grass sparkled. Once again, the village people rose from rest and started preparing for the day's activities. Wives were making breakfast, and men were getting ready to go to their jobs.

Children were getting dressed for school; all the while, there was talk and laughter and eating. Soon the men departed for their jobs, and the children left their homes to walk to school.

Some days passed with activity in the village of Salem and with activity up on the old hill. Finally, it was October 31, and the children were extremely excited. Their parents had planned for them to go trick-or-treating about the village later that night.

Women were busy making cakes and candies. Tables were lined with covered candy apples, and Halloween baskets were being made. Worn-out old bedsheets were made into ghost costumes, and old clothes from years before were being gathered for the children to wear.

Up on the old hill outside the village, the witch was awake and making plans to ruin Halloween. The witch's crew of friends was busy going about their business around the old house. Charlie the bat was still thinking about how he was going to foil the witch's plot to destroy Halloween.

He knew that he had to come up with something quickly as Halloween night was fast approaching. Charlie hid out of sight from the rest in the house, thinking harder than ever before.

Charlie wiggled his wings and scratched his furry little head. "I have to do something to stop the witch's plan," he said to himself quietly. Charlie suddenly had the idea to sneak out of the house. He thought that, maybe if he went to the village, he could come up with better ideas. While no one in the house was paying attention to him, he snuck up and out of the chimney.

Quickly Charlie the bat flew down the hill and into the village. When he arrived in the village, he caught sight of the children playing outside. Their parents were working together in preparing the village for Halloween night.

The candles were being lit inside the jack-o'-lanterns, and other candles were being lit too. Small metal lanterns were being set up so that they could be carried about the village as the children went trick-or-treating.

Charlie flew into a nearby tree and watched the people of the village. Charlie wondered if he dared approach the people. He was afraid of being rejected by them as they had rejected the old witch. Charlie swallowed his fear and left the tree. He flew down to the porch of the closest cottage and landed on the rail of the porch.

As the children were scurrying around, one of them caught sight of Charlie. "Oh my, look at the little bat," a young boy said.

The other children gathered around. They looked at Charlie the bat with surprise. A little girl then went over to the bat and patted it on the head ever so gently. "Do you have a name?" the little girl asked.

"My name is Charlie," he said to the little girl.

The little girl put her soft hand over her mouth and giggled quietly. "That is a perfect name for a bat," she said. "My name is Sophia." Charlie looked up at the children and began to smile with nervousness on his face.

The children began to talk among themselves. They wondered if Charlie belonged to the old witch on the hill. Charlie reluctantly replied, "Yes, I do." The parents of the children caught sight of the bat on the rail and went closer to see it.

One of the men looked at Charlie and bent down to get an even closer look at the bat. "You are a cute little bat," the man said. The man continued, "What brings you to our village?"

Charlie looked at everyone standing around and began to nervously share his story. Charlie told the people how the old witch was plotting to ruin Halloween for the children.

The people all gasped in disgust at the story. One of the women put her hands on her hips in disappointment. "What a terrible and cruel thing to do!" she said. Charlie the bat continued explaining the witch's plot.

Then the village people spoke to one another. They started worrying about what they would do to stop the old witch. Charlie flew from the railing where he had been onto a windowsill. Charlie looked at the villagers and the children. "Maybe if we all worked together, we could stop the old witch from ruining Halloween!" So Charlie and the people of the village began to plan together.

Back on the old hill, the witch and her friends had discovered that Charlie was missing. "Where did Charlie go to this time?" Kathy the witch asked herself. The broom, the cat, and the mouse, and Tina began to search all over the house. They looked inside the shoes and even under the shoes. They looked here and there, but Charlie was nowhere to be found.

The day was moving right along, and night was soon to come. So the witch and her crew went over their plans for the night. Tina knew what she was supposed to do, and the others did too. Kathy the witch gathered what was needed to fulfill her vile plot.

The broom, the mouse, the cat, and the bat began to jump around with joy. "We will have much fun ruining Halloween!" they all said together.

The witch and her crew began to get ready to leave the house and to make the trip down the old hill. The sky had begun to get dark now, and the sun was falling out of sight. Owls began to be seen flying to nearby trees. And they could be heard hooting here and hooting over there.

Back in the village, the people had finished making their plans to thwart the witch and her devious plot. The children were also going to help because in a short time they had all come to like Charlie very much. The men and the women liked Charlie too; they knew now that he liked the children.

The moon had risen now in the night sky once again. It was big and yellow and had a passing cloud cutting out its bright light. The stars in the sky glimmered and shimmered. The trees once again began to cast their long and mysterious shadows across the land.

The dry leaves on the ground began to dance freely in the soft fall winds. The wind blew through the bare trees, announcing the arrival of Halloween night.

Now Kathy the witch and her crew left the house on the hill. Carrying homemade lanterns carved out of gourds, they made their way through the thick forest quietly. Down the thin path they went together. The witch's dress would get caught on a stump and sometimes on a fallen, dead tree branch.

Tina the bat rode on the witch's hat, and the mouse and the cat kept close to each other. Mr. Bristles the broom stayed ahead of the crowd, sweeping the path as they went along.

The people and their children went to the edge of the village and stood at the bottom of the old hill. Charlie the bat was leading them because he wanted to make the witch and her crew ashamed of themselves for what they were going to do. Charlie the bat became filled with courage and began to puff himself up a bit.

Down the narrow and winding path, the witch came with her crew closer and closer to the edge of the village. At the same time, the village people stood watch at the bottom of the hill, and they began to see the light from the witch's lanterns. Charlie turned and looked back at his new friends. "She is almost here!" he said.

The village people and their children got ready for the witch and her crew. Pretty soon, into the clearing came Mr. Bristles the broom, sweeping as he had been. Then the witch came into the light of the moon, free from the dark shadows of the thick forest. The cat and the mouse appeared and sat down. Tina the bat stayed on the witch's hat and stretched her wings.

Kathy the witch stared in amazement at the villagers and their children. "Why? What is this I have come upon?" Kathy asked out loud. Then Charlie the bat flew into the air and flew toward the witch, landing on her long and pointed nose.

Charlie landed just so that he could give the witch a good stare right into her eyes. "I'm not going to let you ruin Halloween!" he declared. Charlie stood on the witch's nose with himself puffed up and with his wings flapping.

"Is that so?" Kathy replied, as she stood with Charlie on her nose. Charlie took a step closer to the witch's eyes. "Yes, it is!" he responded. Kathy the witch swatted at Charlie to get him off her long and pointed nose. So he flew off into the air to avoid being swatted.

Charlie took his place now on an old branch that lay just beside the withered and brown grass. He began to explain to the witch and her crew how wrong they were for being so cruel. He continued explaining how the feelings of the people and their children would be hurt.

Charlie looked at Kathy the witch with sadness in his eyes. "Do you really want to see the children cry?" he asked. Kathy the witch looked at the village people and their children and stood for a moment in silence. One of the village women spoke up, saying, "You don't have to be a mean old witch."

Then the woman continued, "We don't like being afraid of you." Then the witch and her crew and the village people, too, all stood in silence for a time. Charlie the bat sat on the branch and began to explain how everyone could get along with one another and how everyone could be happy.

Kathy the witch began to think about what Charlie was saying to her. She stood and looked back at Charlie for a few moments. Kathy then asked what a witch would do if she was not mean and cruel.

The men and the women of Salem moved closer to the witch, and they told the witch that she did not have to be alone on the hill if she was nice. The village people continued to explain how they could make cakes and apple pies for Kathy. The witch thought deep thoughts for a moment, and then a smile started to appear.

Charlie flew from the branch and landed on the witch's cloak and smiled at Kathy the witch. "Please let the children have Halloween," he said to the witch.

Mr. Bristles the broom, the cat, the mouse, and Tina too all looked at Kathy the witch. The witch dropped her lantern and began to cry. "I have been a terrible old witch," she sobbed.

Charlie the bat reached over and wiped the witch's tears from her eyes. "Now, you can be a good witch," Charlie said.

Kathy looked at all the village people and then to her friends from the hill. "I want to have more friends," she said softly.

The village people and their children all moved closer to Kathy and her crew. "We would like that very much," they all said.

With that, the witch threw her things into the woods and told the people and their children that they could have Halloween. Everyone jumped for joy and laughed and carried on.

The children all grabbed one another's hands and formed a big circle around Kathy the witch and began to skip. The broom and the cat and the mouse and Tina the bat started to sing out in joy. The village people began to clap their hands and jump around. The people gathered around Kathy the witch and invited her to their village for treats and fun.

Kathy the witch, with a smile on her face, looked at Charlie the bat. "Thank you so much, Charlie, for showing me how to be a good witch." Kathy stood among all her new friends and was filled with much joy. All the village people and their children turned and headed back to the village.

Kathy and her crew from the hill began to follow them. Charlie the bat flew up into the sky, and he looked down on Kathy with joy in his eyes. All the people from the village welcomed Kathy and the broom and the cat and the mouse and Tina the bat into their cottages.

The children all got dressed in their Halloween costumes and got their baskets and went out trick-or-treating. They went screaming and laughing from cottage to cottage, knocking on doors. Charlie the bat went trick-or-treating with them, and he was happy. In the children's baskets were candy-covered apples and popcorn balls and homemade sugar candies.

The children stayed outside to play, and they invited Charlie to play with them. Laughter and singing filled the night air as the children and Charlie the bat played. Inside the cottages, the village people shared pies and fresh apple cider with Kathy and her crew.

They all talked and shared old stories of Salem. Kathy the witch was so happy, and her friends from the house on the hill were too. Now all was well in the village of Old Salem, and Kathy the witch eventually moved down from off the old hill and built a cottage.

Mr. Bristles got a job sweeping the cottages in the village, and Stinker the cat had children to play with. Cheese the mouse had plenty of crumbs to eat. Tina the bat found a nice hole in a tree to make a home out of, and Charlie the bat was happy.

Every year after that, the village people and the witch and the broom, the cat and the mouse and the bats all got together to celebrate Halloween. Charlie the bat will always be remembered for saving Halloween.

About the Author

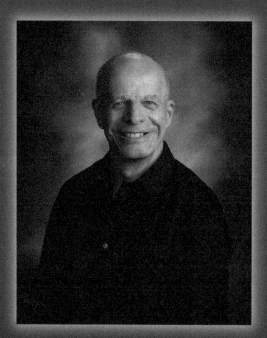

Timothy grew up and worked hard on a small family dairy farm in Upstate New York. In school he loved art class, and he gravitated to drawing and oil painting. Throughout the years, he tried making a living with art, but he had no professional training to help him be successful. One day, Tim decided to try his hand at writing stories, using his imagination as a stepping-stone. For now, Tim is focused on writing enjoyable children's books. As he builds his career as a writer, he may eventually move into other genres.

CPSIA information can be obtained
at www.ICGtesting.com
Printed in the USA
LVHW071631121022
730560LV00006B/148